1 + der + ful

U R A
WINNER

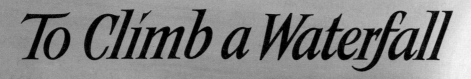

To Climb a Waterfall

JEAN CRAIGHEAD GEORGE

ILLUSTRATED BY
THOMAS LOCKER

PHILOMEL BOOKS
NEW YORK

Philomel Books, a division of The Putnam & Grosset Group,
200 Madison Avenue, New York, NY 10016.
Philomel Books, Reg. U.S. Pat. & Tm. Off.
Published simultaneously in Canada.
Printed in Hong Kong by South China Printing Co. (1988) Ltd.
Book design by Nanette Stevenson. Lettering by David Gatti.
The text is set in Sabon.

Library of Congress Cataloging-in-Publication Data
George, Jean Craighead, 1919-   To climb a waterfall /
Jean Craighead George, Thomas Locker. p.   cm.
Summary: Gives directions for climbing a waterfall,
including where to rest and what to look for.
[1. Waterfalls—Fiction.]   I. Locker, Thomas, 1937-   ill. II. Title.
PZ7.G2933To   1995   [E]—dc20   93-5841   CIP   AC
ISBN: 0-399-22673-7

1   3   5   7   9   10   8   6   4   2

First Impression

To *the children who will climb the waterfall.*

To climb a waterfall, go to the foot of the mountains. Look for a cleft in the skyline and find the stream that cut the cleft. It will be flickering among the trees of the forest as it hunts for the sea.

Walk up the streamside toward the mist that hangs over the canyon of the waterfall.

You will come to a trout pool.
Jump into the cool freshet and swim
against the current like the spirited trout.

Climb out on the rocks. You are in the middle of the tumbling cascades, the home of the waterthrush and otter.

Walk deeper into the canyon. Turn over the rocks.
If you are lucky you'll find a two-lined salamander,
the oldest creature of the waterfall canyon.

The climb becomes steeper, the water wilder.
Look through it at the water pennies that flatten
themselves against the rocks to withstand the current.
Beside them are caddis fly youngsters that hang on
with threads they spin to the rocks.

Take the footpath that leads through the dark forest of the deer.
Hear the thundering roar? Run to the clearing.
There in the sunlight plunges the waterfall.
An artist might be there.

He will probably tell you he has been coming
back to this spot year after year trying to paint
the spirit of the waterfall.
Look.

When you are ready, take to the hemlock path.
Grab their roots and pull yourself up.

Step out on the ledge. A writer might be there composing
a poem about the many sounds of the waterfall.
Listen.

Then go up through the starflowers.
You're not far from the top.

Be as flat as a water penny as you come over the rim
to the sky.

You are there. Stand up.

The waterfall is now part of you.

Take it with you wherever you go,
and you'll never be bored again.

9/26/97
Thank you doctor fritz
for teaching me SRA
and Being nice to me
and testing me thank you
I will miss you. Flo%

Thanks for
everything you
did for us
P.S. Good luck
At Your New
School!
Chris Gerdes

9,26,97
Thank you for helping
me cach up in the 7 grade
I think you very good at
you Job. I think you
one of my best friends

Willie Lawson

Thank you
docter fritz for helping
me during SRA I am
glad I was able to meet you
I think you are real nice
Im gonna miss you.

Sincedly Baty B.
P.S. Good luck

Dakota
I hope you do
good

Thank you for
doing SRA with
us and I saw you Davids.
att the donut shop
Thanks for
being with us